Cole in Her Stocking

A Crossing Forces Christmas

Cole
IN HER STOCKING

USA *Today* Bestselling Author
C.A. SZAREK

Cole in Her Stocking
C.A. Szarek

A Crossing Forces Christmas.

Paper Dragon Publishing
North Richland Hills, TX

eBook ISBN: 978-1-941151-35-8
Print book ISBN: 978-1-941151-36-5

Published in the United States of America
Second eBook Edition: November, 2017
Second Print Edition: November, 2017

Other Books by C.A. Szarek

<u>Crossing Forces — Romantic Suspense</u>

Collision Force (Book One)
Chance Collision (Book Two)
Calculated Collision (Book Three)
Collision Control (Book Four)
Superior Collision (Book Five)

<u>The King's Riders — Epic Fantasy Romance</u>

Sword's Call (Book One) — *Also in Audio!*
Love's Call (Book Two) — *Also in Audio!*
Rogue's Call (Book Three) — *Coming soon in Audio!*
Fate's Call (A Novella from the World of the King's Riders) — *Also in Audio!*

<u>Highland Secrets — Historical Fantasy/Time Travel</u>

The Tartan MP3 Player (Book One)
The Fae Ring (Book Two)
The Parchment Scroll (Book Three)

Highlander's Portrait (A Highland Secrets Story) — *Coming soon to Audio!*
Highland Valentine (A Highland Secrets Story) — *only .99*
The Princess and The Laird (A Highland Secrets Prequel)

Highland Treasures — Historical Fantasy/Time Travel

Highland Oath (Book One) — *Coming January 2018!*
Highland Essence (Book Two) — *Coming soon!*

Anthologies

Deep in the Hearts of Texas — *FREE read!*
   Story: Promise (A Crossing Forces Companion)

Chapter One

"**B**ABY, PLEASE. I don't know what else to do with you."

Micah ignored her plea and let out a wail loud enough to shatter glass.

Andi sighed and changed his position, propping him higher on her shoulder. She slipped onto the couch, trying not to jostle her son too much. Her vision blurred.

He didn't want lulled in the rocker, he wouldn't tolerate the swing, and all hell broke loose if she put him in his crib.

The makers of Baby Ambesol could kiss her ass.

Nothing was working today.

Tears hot on her cheeks, she cried as much as Micah did.

Her son wiggled, so she let him settle on her lap. Big misty blue eyes met her gaze and Andi bit her bottom lip to stave off more tears.

He was hurting, she was frustrated.

Same boat.

Micah whimpered when she smoothed his soft dark curls, but he snuggled into her chest.

She yawned and swiped at her face as his cries softened. She lifted him closer and he buried his little face in her neck. "That's it, Micah. Shhh," she whispered, but the moment she rubbed his back, he started screaming again. Andi groaned. "What d'you want me to do?"

Shoving his whole fist in his mouth, tears fell down his cheeks and her heart broke. His dimples peeked as he gnawed his little knuckles, but her baby wasn't smiling.

Andi grabbed the spit rag that was perma-present on her shoulder and wiped his face.

He leaned away and howled.

She dragged her hand down her face and sniffled.

They'd had a rough night, a rough day—hell, a rough week. She glanced over her son's head at the undecorated Christmas tree that dominated half the living room. Lights weren't even turned on.

Who had time for holiday cheer when one was the mother of *the* most stubborn baby on the planet?

She was no stranger to lack of sleep. Lost count of the nights she'd stayed awake when she and Pete were working a case. But it was different when a screaming infant was the cause.

Exhaustion was always *worse* when it held desperation's hand. Especially when Andi was helpless to comfort her child.

The front door swung open and the deep chuckle of a man accompanied by the chatter of a little boy had her heart leaping.

Relief was short lived as Micah's screams increased, so she scrambled to her feet.

Cole took one look at them and froze under the archway leading into living room. "Awww, babe. The whole time?"

Her lip wobbled as she nodded, her vision blurring again.

Micah turned toward his father's voice and stopped crying, taking big gulps of air and sucking in his bottom lip.

"Mama." Ethan smiled, but his big blue eyes were concerned. "Baby Micah okay?" her four-year-old asked.

"He's fine." Andi's voice shook.

Your mother, on the other hand, is touch and go.

Her husband set his many shopping bags down by the Christmas tree and was at her side in seconds. "Give him here."

She relinquished the squalling baby and sighed.

Micah looked up at Cole and whimpered, but as his father whispered to him and bounced him a bit, the little traitor quieted.

Andi frowned. "I tried that!"

He chuckled, but when his gray eyes met hers, his expression sobered. "It's okay. I got him. Why don't you go catch a few?" Cole pulled her into his chest with his free arm and pressed a kiss to her lips.

Ethan grabbed one of her hands as she rested her head against her husband's chest.

Andi let her eyes slip closed and inhaled his aftershave, mixed with Micah's clean baby scent.

Cole rubbed her back and she pulled their older son to her side, his slender shoulders against her thigh.

She patted his little chest and he pressed a kiss to the back of her hand. Andi smiled. "Thanks, baby. I needed that."

Ethan grinned, then pulled away, dashing to the shopping bags. "Mama, we got ornaments and presents!"

"Buddy, you're not supposed to tell her that," Cole admonished, but he laughed.

Unrepentant, the little boy started to dig in the bags.

Micah sniffled but his dad bounced him, and once again, their baby quieted, sucking on his small fist.

She yawned and shook her head, but kissed his soft cheek and caressed his downy hair.

"Go ahead and nap, babe," Cole whispered. "I got the boys."

"You sure?"

"Yes ma'am." He kissed her. "I'll change and feed him. You need a break."

"I do not." Andi harrumphed.

Her husband smirked and she couldn't bite back a wry smile.

"My stubborn wife. It's okay to let me help you. Thought you would've learned that by now. *My* kids, too."

"I don't want to admit defeat. I should be able to handle him."

Micah gave a loud yawn that made both his parents smile.

"Looks like you wore each other out," Cole said.

"Yeah yeah. See you in a few, then." She made a dismissive gesture. "Ethan, come give me a kiss."

"Hours," Cole muttered, but Andi ignored him.

The little boy rushed to her and she swept him up into her arms, grinning at the loud smack he planted on her cheek. "Be easy on your dad, okay?"

He nodded and slid to the tan carpet, returning to his exploration of the fruits of the shopping trip.

Andi awoke to a delicious scent tickling her nose. She stretched and glanced at the clock. 4:39 glowed in neon blue. She yawned away the remnants of sleep and stared as she oriented.

Oh, yeah. Saturday. Four days before Christmas.

Popping up, she dragged her hand down her face. "Holy crap, I slept for three hours."

She scrambled out of bed, disregarding the jeans she'd slipped out of to take her nap. She folded them, laying the dark denim on the trunk at the end of the king sized bed.

Soft gray sweats caressed her thighs as she pulled them on, and Andi gave into the urge for a nice full body stretch. She felt rested.

Dreaded the evening and overnight if Micah was going to continue his fussy teething routine, but at least she'd caught up on a little bit of shut-eye.

She paused as she opened the bedroom door. Christmas music drifted down the hallway. She cocked her head to one side. The only other thing she could hear was the hum of Cole and Ethan's voices.

No screaming baby.

Was it too much to hope that her husband had coaxed him to sleep?

Andi made her way to the living room.

Her man and older son were decorating the tree; neither noticed her just yet.

She surveyed the room.

Playpen. Small form visible.

Sleeping?

Tiptoeing to the mesh side, she peered in. Her five-month-old was indeed out like a light, his angelic face turned toward her. One small fist was tucked next to his cheek, his onesie-covered rump in the air.

Leaning down, Andi caressed his soft his dark curls.

"Hi, Mama! Look!" Ethan grinned, holding up a small teddy bear Christmas ornament that displayed a number pale blue number two.

She straightened and smiled. "I see. Your two-year-old ornament."

Ethan nodded and turned toward the fluffy fake evergreen. Although he didn't place it very high, he carefully attached the hook to the tree.

"Good job, buddy," she said.

"Hey, babe." Cole flashed dimples that made her heart trip over itself. He was at her side in seconds, pulling her into his arms and pressing a kiss into her lips.

Andi sighed into his embrace, suddenly wishing they were alone, sans children. *Naked* would be good, too. They'd both been so tired because the baby wasn't sleeping; it'd been a while. "Hi," she whispered into his mouth.

Steel eyes darting to Ethan, he kissed her once more, but the quick brush of his lips wasn't nearly enough. "Later. But definitely tonight. *Really.*" His gaze was intense.

At least they were on the same page.

"I want you," he whispered in her ear.

Shivering, she nodded and stayed close, reveling in his arms around her and the hard muscles of his chest.

"Something smells good." Andi needed a distraction to tamp down her rising libido.

"Lasagna in the oven."

She smirked, and pulled back to meet his eyes. "Going for Super Dad *and* Husband-of-the-Year?"

"Yeah, but don't tell anyone." One corner of his mouth shot up.

Andi grinned. "Oh yeah, Detective Lucas would never live that down."

Cole chuckled.

"Mama, wanna help?" Ethan called, taking more of his favourite ornaments out of the large red and green sorter.

"Yes, sir." She bit back a yelp when her husband smacked her butt. Her mock-glare only got her another flash of dimples. Andi shook her head, but couldn't keep the grin off her face.

"I love you," he mouthed, whistling and moving back to the tree. He arranged the fat globe lights she'd had him add to their pre-lit tree.

"I'll get you later," she muttered, ignoring his laugh as she squatted down next to her son.

"Hope so," Cole answered, waggling his eyebrows before ducking out of sight behind fake evergreen.

She laughed, ruffling Ethan's copper curls when he grinned and handed her an angel from the box.

They decorated the tree as a family, something Cole had declared was a new tradition for them. It was Micah's first Christmas, but it was also their first Christmas as a family.

Her man must've been deprived all those years on his own, because Christmas was suddenly a big deal around the MacLaren-Lucas household. It was great to watch him having so much fun, especially with the boys.

Andi's former FBI agent husband had been working a case last Christmas, and undercover the one before. He'd lived alone in New York City the whole time he'd worked for the Bureau.

She grinned as she watched them together, laughing as her tall husband lifted their son to place the angel on the top of the seven foot tree. At six foot four, even without Ethan, Cole didn't need a stepladder.

The phone rang and she glanced over her shoulder.

Cole groaned as he set the little boy to his feet. He and his partner, Jared Manning, were the on-call detectives for the entire week of Christmas.

"Don't worry. It can't be work. They would've called your cell."

"True," he said.

Making a dash for the cordless, Andi hit the *talk* button without looking at Caller ID. A fit of coughing greeted her ear before she could even say hello, but the cough-voice was familiar. "Mom?"

More coughing amongst a croaked, "Yes."

"Mom, are you okay?" She frowned.

Her mother and step-dad, Ed, lived in Ohio. *And* were supposed to be on a plane to Texas in the morning.

"Hi, baby," her mom, Debbie, said. Heavy congestion obscured her normal tones.

"You don't sound so good."

"I'm not."

Dread settled over Andi. "What's wrong?"

"Ed and I have the flu. Fevers, the shakes, vomiting, the works. We're not going to be able to come."

"Aww, Mom. It's Christmas."

"I know, baby. I know. And I really wanted to see you guys. But even if we came, we'd just infect the whole family."

Swallowing the lump in her throat, she nodded even though her mother couldn't see her. She bit her lip to stave off tears.

They hadn't seen her mom and her second husband since Micah was born.

"Okay."

Cole shot her a look at her shaky tone, so she turned away from her husband and son. Neither of them needed to know she was close to tears.

"Can you come next week or something?"

I need your help with my screaming baby.

"Well, Ed's already been out of the office over a week. You know how he fusses."

"Mom, he's the boss. It's his company."

Her mother sighed and Andi clutched the phone tighter.

What's wrong with you?

Crying for her mother at thirty-two years old?

"I'll see what we can do. As soon as we feel better."

Her stomach sank to her toes at the same time guilt crept up. She hadn't even focused on the fact her mother felt horrible. "I'm sorry. I really hope you feel better. It's just…I wanted to see you. I love you."

"Oh, I know, baby. I love you, too."

"Cass, Dale and the kids couldn't get away, either. They're coming after New Year's. Maybe we could time it so we're all together."

"We'll see. It won't be Christmas without you."

Andi almost choked on the lump in her throat. Had to force polite words out. "Get better, Mom. I miss you."

"I miss you, too, and those grandbabies. Kiss them for me. And give Cole my love. I need to go. Ed's hollering for me."

"Okay, Mom. Say hello to Ed and give him our love, too. Merry Christmas." She hung up, dropped the phone in its cradle, and sighed. "Guess it's just us for Christmas."

Chapter Two

C OLE'S HEART THUMPED at the disappointment in his wife's expression. What was wrong with *just them* for Christmas? A quiet family thing, with her and their boys, was right up his alley.

He liked his in-laws all right, but still. He'd miss his sister, the girls, and even his brother-in-law, but they'd see them in a few weeks, and it wasn't like he hadn't missed out on his nieces opening presents before. Well, like every year for the last…six or seven.

Andi was having a hard time admitting their baby was taking it out of her, so he understood she wanted her mom, but what was he, chopped liver?

He'd been up just as many an overnight, midnight feedings, diaper changes and just plain comforting Micah as she had.

How many times did he have to tell her '*my kid, too.*'?

All that aside, Cole wanted to comfort his wife. "C'mere, babe."

Andi buried her face against his neck as soon as his arms were around her.

He inhaled her strawberry scented shampoo, squeezing her against him and closing his eyes. Cole held her as she sniffled into his shirt. He rubbed her back in wide soothing circles like he'd done when she was pregnant with Micah.

Trying to hide tears was so like Andi.

"Hey, listen. It'll be okay. We'll have an awesome Christmas," he whispered.

She met his gaze, blue eyes misty. "I know. I feel like an ass for being upset. I *am* looking forward to Christmas with you and our boys. Really, I am."

He smiled and kissed her, brushing a stray lock of chestnut hair out of her face. "You're not an ass, babe. Sucks about your mom and Ed, though. What happened?"

"They have the flu. Mom sounded bad."

"No Grandma and Grandpa Ed?" Ethan's bottom lip trembled.

Great.

If their son cried, it'd be even worse on his wife.

"They're sick, baby," Andi told him.

"What about my presents?"

Cole bit back a laugh; he'd let her handle this one.

"They'll come as soon as they can. They don't want to get us sick, too." She wiggled out of his arms, squatting in front of their four-year-old, admonishing him it wasn't nice to worry about presents before ill grandparents.

He couldn't help but notice how the cotton of her sweats clung to her ass and stretched over muscled thighs. On full display as she rested one knee on the carpet.

Cole swallowed, shifting on his feet and trying to convince his cock now wasn't the time. He was tired of being too exhausted to make love to his wife. Cold showers sucked ass and his hand did nothing for him anymore.

He wanted Andi naked in his arms, her back arched, blue eyes hazy with passion. Screaming his name as he tasted her.

Knock it off. That's soooo not for right now.

He didn't need tight jeans in front of his kids.

Micah whimpered from the playpen and Cole jumped on the distraction. He hurried across the room and looked down at his son.

Stirring from sleep, the little one yawned and he grinned, leaning down to scoop him up.

The baby wormed his small warm body into Cole's chest, and he held his breath while he waited for the scream that never came.

He didn't hold back a sigh.

Relief was written all over Andi's face when their eyes met. She straightened, smoothing Ethan's red hair before coming over to him and Micah.

"He's awake. And *not* screaming his lungs out. There is a God," she said.

"I won't say anything to jinx us, then."

"Please don't."

Cole grinned and rubbed Micah's tiny back. He glanced at the clock on the cable box. "Dinner's ready."

After not having *normal* for longer than he could remember, he craved the little things. Dinner with Andi and Ethan, talking to them both in the bright kitchen of the house that had slipped from hers to *ours* not long after he'd come back to Texas.

He set Micah in his carrier and held his breath as Andi set the table.

Please don't scream.

Blinking wide blue eyes, his son grinned and his shoved his fist in his mouth, drool rolling down his little chin.

"Does he need a teething ring? There're a few in the freezer." She grabbed two oven mitts.

"He's okay for now. Babe, I was going to do that. You should take it easy."

Andi flashed a smile that made his stomach flutter and his cock twitch.

"I want to do this. You made dinner."

"Do I lose points if I admit it's the freezer-section variety?" He winked.

She laughed as she lowered the oven door. "Like I've just met you? I figured. But I thought you might've ordered in. I love *Rizzoli's* lasagna."

Cole chuckled. "Sorry, not this time. You still love me anyway?"

Her blue eyes locked onto his and her full mouth parted. "Always." The teasing was gone from her expression and his heart tripped.

"Daddy, can I have milk?" Ethan's voice broke the spell and his wife whirled the other direction with a wink, hipping the oven door closed.

"Of course, bud." Making quick work of the kid's request, he set the colorful mug on the table in front of the boy.

"Thank you!"

The both laughed at their older son's enthusiasm at the same time.

Cole helped her serve their supper, cutting the garlic bread and setting it on three plates before she took hers and Ethan's to the table. He grabbed his own and followed.

Their eyes met as they both took a seat.

He grabbed her hand, bringing it to his mouth to press a kiss to her knuckles. "I'm glad you took vacation this week."

She smiled. "I'm glad you did, too. Too bad Chief roped you into being on-call as a part of the deal. Now if only your cell doesn't ring."

"Oh, babe." Cole groaned. "You know you just jinxed us."

"Nah." Andi shook her head.

Micah kicked his little feet and made cooing noises. His movements made the toys dangling on the handle of his carrier jingle. The baby giggled.

"Wow. I almost want to ask where my kid went. Just who is this happy baby?" Cole teased, grabbing his younger son's little foot and shaking it until Micah cooed again.

"Don't you dare say that!" Her expression was mock-outraged. "I like Happy-Micah better than Screamy-Micah."

"Me, too!" Ethan announced.

He chuckled.

Ethan shoved lasagna in his mouth, sauce on his little cheek.

Andi shook her head and admonished him to wipe his face, but he did it, so she didn't have to.

He held his fork backwards as he went in for more dinner, but allowed his mother to turn the utensil and remind him how to stab the noodles she'd already cut up. The little boy flashed a grin before taking another bit.

Glad he's happy tonight, too.

A smile played at Cole's lips. Ethan had already grown so much since he'd come back, married Andi and moved in. It was a wonder to see. He only had more to look forward to.

With both his sons.

Evening faded into night, and he put Micah down after a bottle so Andi could read a story to Ethan following his bath.

Falling into the rhythm of parenting should've been the hardest thing he'd ever done, but it wasn't. Cole had found his niche.

He thrived at being a father.

Sitting in the rocker with his child in his arms was something he wouldn't trade for anything in the world. A nightly ritual that only made him feel better with time.

He stared down into Micah's crib, watching the little guy sleep for a few moments. His heart stuttered at the innocent perfection before him.

Why had he always thought he'd never want this?

Damn good thing love had changed *everything*.

Now that he had it, he'd never let it go.

Not Andi, Ethan or Micah.

Andi's arms slipped around his waist and he fought the urge to jump. He hadn't heard her enter the room.

"Sorry," she murmured. "Didn't mean to startle you." Her lips on his neck combined with her breasts pressing into his back shot bolts down his spine.

Cole pulled her around to the front of his body, cradling her against his chest. His cock stirred to half-mast, throbbing as her warm clean breath caressed his cheek. "We should go to the bedroom. Now."

"Why?" Humor wrapped her words, and she rocked into him, tearing a groan from his lips.

"Because I don't want to strip you down in front of one of the boys, even if he's only five months old."

Andi laughed. It was throaty, sexy, and told him she knew *exactly* how crazy she was about to make him. She took his hand without another word and practically dragged him to their master suite.

At least they were on the same page. Cole wanted her — no, *needed* her. Was starved for her. His palms itched to touch her, his tongue burned to taste her.

Damn, calm down.

He was going to come in his jeans if he didn't get a hold of himself. The zipper cutting into sensitive skin only made him want her more.

Then again, it was always like this with her. Control wavered. Desire and love made his blood boil for Andi.

His wife. Love of his life.

"Cole? You okay?" She glanced over her shoulder, her hands at the bottom of her shirt.

"Be better when you're naked, babe."

She flashed a grin. "Look who's talking."

His heart did another flip-flop and he yanked his tee up and over his head.

Andi's lips on his neck and fingers on the fly of his jeans jolted him as much as her naked breasts teasing his bare pecs.

His lovely wife had wasted no time losing her bra along with her shirt.

Cole let her push his jeans and boxer briefs off his hips. Then he took over, shoving them down and slipping out of socks and shoes. He left the denim in a pile right there on the carpet, his eyes glued to Andi's intense blue gaze.

She was devouring him, and she hadn't even touched him yet.

His cock pulsed and he groaned. "Andi."

Her eyes shot to his face and she licked her lips.

Actually licked her lips.

He fought a shiver and the tightening in his balls.

She's gonna frickin' kill me.

"I need you," she whispered.

Cole tugged her into his arms and took her mouth. Couldn't agree more, but showing was better than telling.

Andi moaned and kissed him back hard, rocking her cotton sweats into his pelvis.

He tugged them off one hip. "Off. Now."

She smirked but took a step back, shimmying out of pants and panties.

Cole stared—couldn't help it. His wife was the most beautiful woman he'd ever seen.

But she squirmed and moved to cover herself.

"Babe, what're you doing?" he whispered, taking her wrists and gently moving them away from her body.

Andi blushed and looked away. "My stretch marks have stretch marks. I don't know how you can look at me like that. I lost the baby weight, but…my body is different."

Cupping her cheeks, he forced her to meet his eyes. "Mine. Your body is mine. You're *mine*. You are gorgeous and this body gave me Micah." He caressed her shoulders, her breasts and her hips, the place she was most self-conscious of. "I love you. And my heart, my body, is *yours*." He pressed her hand flat to his chest over his heart.

She offered a watery smile. "I love you, too." Her whisper was wobbly, her eyes misty. Her pink cheeks and kiss-swollen lips made him burn for her even more.

"Now can I have you?"

Andi laughed and he grinned when she wrapped her arms around his neck. "You'll always have me. But you can *take* me now."

Cole nipped her earlobe and swung his wife up into his arms. "I won't have you crying, unless it's to scream my name."

Her cheeks reddened again as their eyes met, her freckles prominent.

He kissed her cheekbones before setting her at the center of their bed and following her down. Cole took her mouth as she wrapped herself around him; their bodies touched in all the right places. He wanted to make sweet slow love to her, but was too eager. Slow and tender would have to wait. He needed inside her.

Now.

Good thing his wife had the same idea. Andi rubbed her hips into his, and his cock jumped.

He groaned and dragged his fingertips across her sex. A quick glance down told him she was already swollen and glistening for him. He parted her folds to feel her slickness, and bit his bottom lip to keep from moaning.

Cole rubbed her clit until she squirmed.

"Please…" Andi begged.

Positioning himself, he thrust forward, filling her in one long stroke.

She gasped and snaked her arms around his neck, pulling him down.

He didn't miss the invitation to kiss her when she tilted her face up. He captured her lips, winding their tongues together as he tasted her.

She kissed him hard, deeper, exploring his mouth as he plundered hers. Andi moved with him, each lunge more frantic than the last.

They were both covered in sweat. Her nails bit into his ass, but he got lost in the rhythm of their bodies until the pleasure was too much.

His spine tingled, his balls tightened. He was so close.

She cried out, arching her back and hanging onto him as her whole body contracted. Her heels dug into his ass, but he didn't care.

Cole held her tight to his chest, face buried in her neck as his cock throbbed inside her, shooting his release deep. Her inner muscles tightened in waves and a tremor shot down his spine as the pleasure intensified.

Andi kissed him again, her body relaxing into their bed, and he followed her lead as his softening erection slipped from her body.

She panted in his arms, her heartbeat thundering against his.

"I love you," Cole croaked. He took a deep breath, his head still spinning.

"I love you, too." She smiled and squeezed her arms around him.

"Let me move, babe. I don't want to crush you."

His wife always wrapped herself around him after they made love. She never wanted to let him go.

"I like your weight on top of me," Andi whispered, but loosened her hold.

He chuckled. "So you always tell me. But I don't want to hurt you."

"You never hurt me."

Cole smiled and stood from their bed. "Be right back." After a quick kiss, he jogged to the bathroom to get a warm wet cloth. He cleaned himself up and did the same to Andi when he returned to her.

She wiggled. "That tickles."

Laughing again, he skimmed his fingertips over her sex.

Andi shivered and made a grab for his wrist, but he was too fast, and repeated his move. Her flesh was still swollen and contracted under his touch.

Damn, she was so hot.

"You're evil."

Shaking his head, Cole tossed the wash cloth in the nearest clothes basket and crawled back into bed with his wife. "That wasn't a tease, babe. It was a promise. I'm nowhere done with you tonight."

She laughed and kissed him in answer.

Chapter Three

ANDI TRACED HIS abs with her index finger until his muscles jumped. "Did I ever tell you, you're hot?"

Chuckling, Cole winked. "I think you may have mentioned it. But you're hotter than me."

She met his eyes and cupped his face, caressing his stubble with both thumbs. "I love you."

His stomach fluttered. Her sapphire eyes were deep pools of emotion. Love, heat, and everything that Andi was stared back at him. "I love you, too."

She smiled and leaned up for a kiss that melted into something more.

He cradled the back of her neck and took control. Their tongues danced, and dueled. Reluctantly he pulled away, in need of a breath.

She sighed into his mouth and rested her forehead against his.

They didn't speak, but they didn't need to.

He smiled as she spread noisy kisses all over his face.

Cole grabbed her sides and tickled her until she squirmed and they both sank into the sheets in a fit of laughter, Andi sprawled across his chest.

"Work didn't call at all. Weird, huh?" she asked, breaking the companionable silence that'd slipped over them.

"Maybe the criminals are taking the holidays off, too."

Grinning, she lifted her head and arched an eyebrow. "Antioch might be small town Texas, but not likely, my love. You and Jared just got lucky tonight."

"Then I hope we stay lucky. Christmas miracle anyone?"

"If only. A Christmas miracle could get my mom and Ed feeling better and down here." Her forehead knitted and she rested her cheek on his right pec.

Cole sighed and rubbed her back. Her skin was warm, supple and tempting beneath his palm. "Christmas will be awesome. You know that, right?"

"I know." But Andi echoed his sigh and her voice was heavy, as if she was trying to convince herself.

He ignored how his heart stuttered. Didn't want her to catch on to how much it meant that they were sharing their first Christmas together as a family.

The last thing he wanted was for her to feel guilty for being upset about her parents. She never liked last minute changes anyway, let alone something as big of a deal as Christmas.

However, if she discovered how much he'd rather it just be her, him and the boys, she'd feel horrible for wanting more.

That type of thing was totally his wife. Cole just wanted to show her she'd always have him. He'd *always* be there for her.

"C'mere." He kissed the top of her head as he pulled her closer. Her heavy breasts brushed his abs when she shifted against him and his cock stiffened.

The need to converse faded and his blood heated, well on its way to a slow boil when her hands started to roam his body.

Cole wanted Andi again.

Her heavy-lidded blue eyes told him she'd read his mind. She scooted up his body and met his mouth half-way.

His hands slipped to her waist to help her straddle him. His cock was granite by the time her delectable ass brushed it. Her hot center sliding along his shaft made his balls ache as she finally settled her sex against his, but he wasn't in the right place.

He needed inside her.

She entwined their fingers and he raised his arms to give her some leverage, but when Andi only ground her hips into his, he growled.

With a smirk, she leaned down to tease his nipples with hers.

His were already peaked; Cole shivered from head to foot. His pulse thundered in his ears. "Babe, you don't want to do that."

"Oh?" Breath exited her mouth on a whoosh when he lifted his hips and rubbed into her from underneath.

His lovely wife fell onto his chest, where he took full advantage of her captured hands. Cole kissed her while grinding his pelvis into her, hitting the sensitive bundle of nerves at the top of her sex. Knowing Andi, it wasn't enough friction for her to orgasm, but it was a hell of a tease.

"Evil," she panted and nipped his bottom lip.

He groaned. "Let me inside and I'll make it all better."

She threw her head back and moaned his name, lifting her ass, only to come back down on him, impaling herself with no guidance from hands. She didn't need the assistance.

They knew each other's bodies well.

He slid into her to the hilt.

They both gasped, but Andi kissed him and started to ride him with a slow rocking rhythm. When she undulated, Cole thrust high and hard, pushing against her hands.

She whispered his name again, but got the message, increasing the pace of her thrusts.

He released her and settled his hands at her slender waist, lifting her up and down when she started to tire. Cole sat up and cradled her on his lap as the sex pounded on.

Andi bent her knees into the bed and circled her hips as she moved against him. Her inner muscles fluttered around him; she was close.

When her head fell back for the second time, he kissed her throat. He thrust one last time.

Her sex squeezed his like a vise and orgasm roared over them both. She whimpered and kissed him hard, gripping his shoulders, shuddering in his arms.

Their mouths parted and Andi buried her face against his neck.

They breathed hard, chest against breasts, and Cole didn't want to be parted from her body; wished his dick was ready to go for round three. He cradled her close, kissing her damp forehead, her cheeks, then the top of her head before pressing a tender kiss to her lips.

"We should get some Z's." Andi's whisper was heavy; she was almost asleep.

They snuggled down into the bed, and he yanked the blankets over them. "Sleep, babe. I'll hold you."

"You sleep, too." She yawned.

Cole smiled. "I will, don't worry."

"Surprised Micah let us have this much time uninterrupted."

"We had a *'Daddy needs Mommy-time'* pep talk."

She lifted her head from his chest, flashing a lopsided grin that made his stomach flutter. "Right. Sure you did."

"Well, I can't leave it to luck, can I babe?"

Andi laughed and kissed his chest before settling against him.

Minutes later, her breathing fell into a deep even rhythm as he rubbed her back. Contentment settled over him, and he didn't fight his yawn.

The look on her face when her mother had broken the news crept up from his memory.

Cole frowned. He didn't want Andi to worry about anything, especially Christmas.

Of course, she could be sad her parents had had to cancel but *he* would be there. The boys would be there. *They* were her family, too. Most important family, actually.

Even after marriage and a baby, Andi didn't rely on him as much as he'd like. She took too much on herself. It was in her make-up to be the strong female, detective, mother, wife.

Still, he wanted to remind her he'd always be there for her. They might not be partners at the police department, but they sure as hell were at home.

Cole sighed and kissed her forehead when she made a noise in her sleep.

They'd have a fantastic Christmas—as a *family*.

He'd just have to show her.

Chapter Four

"I'LL BE BACK, babe."

Andi looked up from the sugar cookies she and Ethan were icing. Well, she was icing them, her son was making a red and green sticky mess, but he was adorable. "Work call?"

"Nope, just need to run out." Cole had an odd expression on his face, but when their eyes met, her husband flashed dimples.

That smile always scrambled her brains—and he knew it.

She studied him, but got nothing. Which made her even more suspicious.

Cole was up to something.

Is it something to do with last night?

He'd helped her get the boys in bed, and right when she'd slipped into comfortable sleepwear, he'd announced he had to go out. Told her not to wait up for him.

Her husband had been evasive when she'd questioned him. Had only explained his partner needed him. Andi hadn't asked much more. Detective Jared Manning had a penchant for spending too much time at the local cop hangout, a bar called *McAuley's*.

Cole had probably had to get him home and cleaned up. Not a responsible thing to do when one was on call, though.

"Jared, okay?"

"Yeah." He paused, as if he didn't know why she was asking.

She narrowed her eyes. "It's Christmas Eve, where could you possibly have to go?"

One dark eyebrow shot up. "I'll never tell. C'mon, don't interrogate me. You're gonna ruin it."

"Hmmm a surprise?"

"A surprise! A surprise!" Ethan jumped off the step stool he'd been using at the counter.

One icing container went flying. Green splats hit the tiled floor.

"Oh, Ethan," Andi groaned.

Cole laughed. "On that note, see you later, babe."

"Of course," she muttered. When Andi looked up, he'd already disappeared from the entryway. The front door closed with a *thump.*

Damn man.

Her son's blue eyes were misty when their gazes brushed. He held his little hands out. "Sorry, Mama."

"It's okay, baby. We have more." She bent and cleaned up the thick blobs of green. Andi righted the icing container and set it on the counter. She rinsed a washcloth in warm water and cleaned her son's hands and face. "Let's try to get some icing *on* the cookies, okay?"

Ethan flashed a grin. "It tastes good, Mama."

"I know, baby. You're going to bounce off the walls all night from all this sugar."

"Bounce, bounce, bounce." He punctuated his words by hopping across the kitchen back to his stool.

Andi found herself laughing, despite the irritation at her delinquent husband. What on earth could he be up to? A last minute gift for her?

They'd agreed to keep the budget reasonable, spending most of their Christmas money on the boys. However, Andi had asked for a few things, and of course, had bought Cole most of the things on his short list.

She'd had to yank it out of him anyway. He'd kept telling her he had everything he needed, but she'd made him name a few items. Everyone should have a present or two to open on Christmas morning.

"Santa's coming tonight?" The excitement in her four-year-old's voice made her grin.

"Yes, sir. After you and Micah go to bed."

"Yay!"

His loud voice made her wince, and Andi shot a look to the baby, napping in his carrier on the kitchen table. The five-month-old didn't stir.

Thank God.

Micah had actually slept through the night. One of the offending teeth had broken through his gums, so perhaps the worst was over.

Andi could hope, anyway.

"I want lotsa presents!" Ethan grinned and slathered red icing on a stocking shaped sugar cookie with a child-sized bladeless tool. He'd gotten it mostly on the treat, so she didn't admonish him.

She encircled him on the stool, and took his small wrist, guiding his hand around the cookie. "There you go, baby. Good job. It looks yummy."

He smiled up at her. "I like making cookies with you, Mama."

Andi kissed the top of his head. "I do, too. Let's do more." She grabbed a snowflake and reached for the white icing.

"Daddy got an owie," Ethan said about ten minutes later, when she was stacking iced cookies in a plastic container with sheets of wax paper between them.

"What, baby?"

"On his arm. A big boo boo."

She looked into his eyes. "A boo boo?"

The little boy nodded and grabbed his upper arm. "Right here."

Her stomach jumped, but she didn't want Ethan to realize he'd raised her alarm. "What did his owie look like?" She kept her voice even, her words slow.

"All white."

All white? A bandage of some sort? Damn.

Had something happened last night between Cole and Jared at *McAuley's*? "Your dad's okay, baby." Andi wanted to question him further, but didn't.

Cole had been dressed and feeding Micah when she'd risen that morning. She'd slept deeply, hadn't woken when he'd come to bed. So she'd had no chance to see his unclothed body. Unless he'd done that on purpose. Something had happened and her husband hadn't wanted her to see a wound.

She swallowed back a curse and reminded herself she couldn't kill Jared Manning. It was Christmas, after all.

Her son's gaze was solemn and innocent, making her heart tripped.

"Daddy's all right, okay buddy?" She ruffled his red curls until he giggled. "Let's get your bath early tonight."

Ethan's little shoulders sank and he pouted like a pro. "Mama, I'm not tired."

"I didn't say bed, now did I? We still have to eat dinner. I said bath. Let's get you unsticky, sugar-boy." Andi tweaked his nose.

"Promise I can stay up?"

"No way. Santa won't come if he thinks you'll see him."

"Awww, Mama."

She bit back a grin at the serious frown on his little face. "We'll put some cookies and milk out for Santa later. And carrots for the reindeer. How about that?"

His face lit up. "Okay!"

"Only if you take a bath now."

Ethan reached for her hand without missing a beat. "Okay, Mama."

Andi laughed.

Chapter Five

COLE SNUCK INTO the living room, setting the long slender box under the Christmas tree behind a big colorful packaged addressed, *To: Ethan, From: Santa.* The gift for Andi was wrapped in simple silver paper and would be the last he offered.

He didn't want her to spot it until then.

His arm smarted with the movements, but his two-day-old tattoo looked awesome this morning. Damn, it'd been difficult to keep it a secret. Who knew his wife expected him to parade around without clothes on?

She'd been extremely suspicious when he'd sported a T-shirt before bed the night before.

Guess that's what you get for marrying a cop.

Cole smirked.

He'd had to tell her he'd needed to finish up a report on his laptop before he could sleep. He'd waited until after midnight, put all the '*From: Santa*' presents for the boys under the tree and gone to bed only after she'd fallen asleep.

Andi was light sleeper, so he'd held his breath as he'd slipped beneath the comforter, but she hadn't woken. She'd snuggled close, her gorgeous body sleep-warmed and soft, but he'd contented himself with just holding her until sleep had claimed him as well.

"Santa came, Santa came!" Ethan hopped down the hallway in his snowman pyjamas.

Cole grinned when he straightened, meeting his older son by the tree. "Breathe, kiddo." He gathered the ball of excitement disguised as a child into his arms.

Andi laughed and shook her head as she joined them, Micah in her arms.

Their baby was awake and smiling.

His wife's gaze swept up and down his body. "Since when do you wear a robe?"

He shrugged and hurried forward to press a kiss to her mouth. "Merry Christmas, babe."

From his perch on Cole's hip, Ethan kissed his mother's cheek at the same time. "Merry Christmas, Mama!"

Her face relaxed into a smile and Cole kissed the baby's dark head before backing away. He sucked in a breath. He'd reveal his surprise in due time.

His suspicious little wife would have to be kept busy with kids and presents so he could get away with it.

"Wanna see what Santa brought, E-man?" Cole asked.

"Yeah!" His older son practically jumped from his arms.

"Hold on, I want to grab the camera," Andi said. "In addition to phone pics, I want some real ones for the scrapbook."

"I already got it."

"Oh, thanks!" She smiled again and they gathered around the tree, all taking a seat on the carpet.

Micah cooed and grinned from his seat on her lap, flashing his one bottom tooth.

Cole grabbed a wiggly Ethan and made him sit to wait and be handed gifts instead of diving under the tree as the kid would have preferred.

"Who's first?" Andi asked.

"Me! Me!" Ethan bounced from his seat and clapped his little hands.

He chuckled and grabbed the closest box for his older son that wouldn't reveal his surprise for his wife.

Chunks of wrapping paper littered the living room carpet.

Ethan had already sped off to his room to play with his dozen new toys.

Cole wanted a moment alone with Andi, so he didn't admonish the little boy to stay in the living room for the sake of Christmas family time.

They had all day together.

Micah napped on a cozy Santa printed Christmas blanket and there were only a few things left under the tree.

His heart had jumped with every picture Andi had snapped and every smile they'd exchanged. Seeing Ethan's excitement would never be seconded.

The contentment and love on his wife's face made him feel like he owned the world.

She was the most beautiful woman he'd ever seen.

"Thanks for the sweater, I really like it." Andi smiled yet again as she folded the red fluffy V-necked garment her friend Nikki had picked out when he'd sought female help. She put it back in the gift box and slid it under the tree.

Nerves churned the coffee in his stomach. Cole was glad they'd planned breakfast after presents; he would've tossed his eggs for sure. He chided himself to calm down.

This is Andi, not a stranger.

She'd love what he'd had made for her. Would know how much it meant — to them both — the moment her eyes rested on it.

But what would she think about the *permanent* part of his gift?

"Hey, you okay?" Andi scooted closer, studying him.

He cleared his throat. "I am. I have one more thing for you."

"Oh?"

Nodding, he kissed her quickly and grabbed the silver package.

"You got quiet on me," she said as she accepted the slender box.

"I'm cool—fine. I'm great. Open it." Cole smiled and his heart thundered as she flipped the present over.

"Jewelry?" She winked and slowly peeled the paper back.

Too slowly.

"You're killin' me, babe."

"Why?" She paused. "Afraid I won't like it?"

"Andi." He mock-glared.

She grinned and ripped the paper off the box so fast it was reminiscent of Ethan. Andi's gasp made his stomach flip. "Oh, Cole." When she met his eyes, hers were misty.

"Do you like it?" His voice cracked.

Andi nodded, one tear slipping down her cheek.

Cole wiped it away.

She cradled the white gold chain in her palm, tracing the oversized links at the front. Her expression was tender. His wife sucked in a breath as she stared at the necklace he'd special ordered from the only jeweler in Antioch. The man had made it himself. Custom, and beautiful.

One-of-a-kind, like Andi.

Their names each had a link. *'Ethan'* and *'Micah'* were etched in fancy lettering between *'Andi'* and *'Cole.'*

"I know you usually don't wear any jewelry other than your wedding ring, but—"

She launched herself at him, kissing the words out of his mouth.

Cole took control and deepened their kiss, holding her close.

"I'll wear it every day," Andi breathed against his mouth. "I love it. So much. And I love you." She kissed him again, fast and hard.

He groaned as he made himself pull away. Otherwise he'd throw her down to the carpet and take her, right by the tree. In the interest of kids and Christmas, it wasn't the best idea. "I love you, too. There's more," he whispered.

"I don't need more, I have you." She handed him the necklace. "Put it on for me?" She turned, allowing easier access.

Cole fastened the shiny white gold around her neck, kissing her skin above the clasp. "It's not something for you. It's something for me. But I need to show you."

She met his eyes, one delicate eyebrow arched.

"Just wait." He shifted away, breaking their physical contact.

Andi's blue eyes widened when he loosed the belt on his robe, but he flashed his best dimpled smile and intentionally let the terry cloth slide from one shoulder before the other. The robe pooled at his waist.

She shook her head and giggled at his impromptu play-strip tease, until her eyes latched onto his right biceps. She gasped.

His heart sped into overdrive.

"Oh, Cole." Andi moved back to him.

"It matches your necklace." He swallowed hard. He wanted to explain to her what the tattoo meant to him, but words dissolved as her fingertips brushed his newly inked skin.

Roots.

Cole had worked undercover consistently when he'd been with the FBI, and even though it wasn't unheard of, identifying marks such as tattoos were discouraged.

It was more than that.

Leaving the Bureau, moving to Antioch to be with Andi and Ethan, having Micah. Marrying the love of his life. It was all as permanent as the chain he'd had placed on his arm.

He needed Andi to see that. Believe it. He'd always be there for her.

She'd marked him as much as the guy who'd inked his skin. Their boys had marked him, too. They were in his heart, but each of them had a link with their names for the world to see how he felt about them. He'd even left room for any other children they might have.

The tattoo was a symbol for Cole.

He was happily chained to Andi and their boys.

Forever.

"I know what getting this means to you," Andi whispered, as if she'd read his mind. Her gaze lowered, and she covered his tattoo with her palm. "You never could before, because you hadn't found your place. But now you have."

A sudden lump in his throat almost made him choke on his words. "Looks like my wife knows me well."

A soft smile bloomed on her lips, spreading until she was beaming. She kissed him. "I love it. It's perfect. It's us."

Cole pulled her close. "You're perfect."

She laughed and shook her head. "Not at all. But this Christmas is. All because of you, Cole Lucas."

"I wanted to make it special."

"You totally did." Her expression went playful and she winked. "But I feel like I owe your partner an apology."

"Huh? Jared? Why?"

"Because Ethan saw your arm and I thought somehow he'd got you hurt. I wanted to kick his ass."

He laughed. "Sorry for fibbing, babe. I needed to be stealthy. And you're too smart for your own good."

Andi grinned. "I *am* a detective."

"Jared wasn't really in on it, so don't kick his ass, okay?"

She nodded and moved back into the circle of his arms, her lips hovering over his. "Did I ever tell you I think ink is hot?"

"No. But you can go into it in detail, later."

"Too bad it has to be later."

Just as her mouth brushed his, Micah started to wail from his blanket.

At the same time, Ethan rushed down the hallway with one of his new toys in his little arms. He shouted, "Look, Mama! Daddy, come see!"

They looked at each other and grinned.

"Merry Christmas, babe."

"Merry Christmas. I wouldn't have it any other way."

The End

USA TODAY Bestselling, award winning author of historical and epic fantasy romance, as well as romantic suspense, C.A. loves to dabble in different genres. If it's a good story, she'll write it, no matter where it seems to fit! She's a hopeless romantic and always will be.

Risking it all for Happily Ever After is what she lives by!

C.A. is originally from Ohio, but got to Texas as soon as she could. She's happily married and has a bachelor's degree in Criminal Justice.

She works with kids when she's not writing.

WEBSITE: http://www.caszarek.com
BLOG: http://www.caszarekwriter.blogspot.com/
TWITTER: https://twitter.com/caszarek
FACEBOOK: http://www.facebook.com/caszarek
INSTAGRAM: https://www.instagram.com/caszarek/
GOODREADS:https://www.goodreads.com/author/show/5815085.C_A_Szarek
NEWSLETTER SIGNUP: http://blogspot.us7.list-manage.com/subscribe?u=296abc5983ebc51c1d4d0972b&id=fb22ce93be
EMAIL: ca@caszarek.com

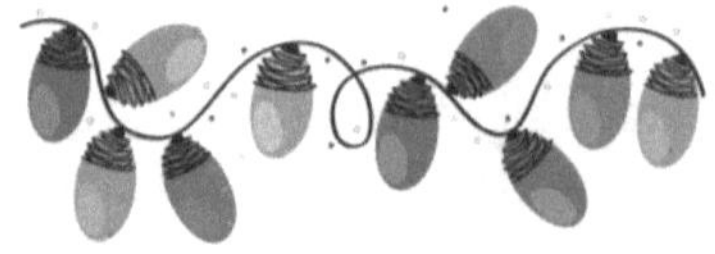

www.ingramcontent.com/pod-product-compliance
Lightning Source LLC
Chambersburg PA
CBHW032044180726
48284CB00008B/2752